DOWN ON FRIENDLY ACRES

Fiddlesticks and gumdrop bars! Welcome to "Down on Friendly Acres," a series based on the life of a real family – my family – the Friend Family. My parents were farmers. They raised crops, livestock and me, along with my two brothers and sister on a farm rightly named Friendly Acres.

Each member of the Friend Family pulled together to do whatever was needed to contribute to daily life. Any one day could consist of baling hay, pulling weeds, shucking corn, feeding the animals, collecting eggs, canning vegetables or even hauling manure.

In the 1960s, a farmer's essential equipment consisted of a tractor, truck, plow, planter, hay baler, corn picker and a manure spreader. Before the 1900's, hauling manure was a back-breaking chore of using a pitchfork to load the manure onto a wagon and then manually distributing the smelly substance in the fields.

The first successful mechanical manure spreader was invented by Joseph Oppenheim in 1899. His new idea came from a paddle ball. The ball (attached to a rubber band) would careen off in different directions dictated by the angle of the paddle. His manure spreader paddles worked much in the same. As a school master, Joseph realized that his invention "The New Idea" would keep his pupils out of the fields and in the classrooms.

Since most of our barns were built before the 1900's, there was no way to back spreaders into them for easy removal of manure. Therefore the manure was manually loaded onto the spreader through a window or door. It didn't take long for the manure to pile up. Before you knew it, the manure would be above your calves (no pun intended). The deeper my rubber boots would sink in the manure, the harder it was to pull myself out to take the next step.

Why bring up such a dirty chore? Because hauling manure has a lot to do with this book on honesty. As a child, it was hard to always tell the truth. Many times I knew if I told the truth, I would get in trouble – big trouble. To get around telling the truth, I'd make up little untruths, digging myself deeper and deeper in a hole. In my attempts to dig myself out I would end up stuck in a mess – much like my rubber boots.

In "Woolly Baaad Lies" I find out the hard way – a lie is a lie is a lie is a lie! If I keep on telling lies, I could eventually turn into a person who couldn't be trusted at all. In this story, telling the truth can be the difference between life and death! Besides, my parents could always spot the "liar's look" a mile away.

Enough with the smelly stuff, one of my fondest memories growing up was raising sheep. Daddy loved his sheep. Involved in Vo-Ag Shows in his youth, he raised a reserve champion ewe.

In the chicken house, during the dead of winter, our ewes gave birth to twins occasionally triplets and once, Ronald, delivered quadruplets. Heat lamps were necessary to keep newborn babies from freezing to death.

I remember how fun it was spending time with those precious newborn lambs. (And yes, my brother's sheep shears story in this book is true.)

Precious times – precious memories – isn't that what life needs to consists of for all of us? My father was born in 1922 and in 2009 went to heaven. I miss him. It is those precious times and precious memories that keep me motivated to share these stories with you. My father loved his animals, his farm, his God, his children and his wife (and yes, The Toot story is even true).

My father spoke not so much in words but in his deeds. He was a giver – planted more than we could ever eat but that's because he loved giving it away. He was a friend - not because his name was Friend but because he loved people. He was a lover of life to the fullest – loved because he loved to love – not because he wanted to be loved. His actions spoke louder than words. The song, "My Father Loves," comes from my heart because of the way my father lived his life!

Anyone who knew my father knew he loved to talk! Anyone who knew my father knew that "he not only talked the talk, he walked the walk!"

Fiddlesticks and gumdrop bars – I've run out of room again. Remember,

I'M A FRIEND
and U R 2!

R. Friend

DEDICATION

. . . in memory and honor of my father, Harold Eugene Friend, for an array of honorable achievements during his eighty-six years on this earth.

. . . for being a father who "taught me what true love is – he shows me how to live – no need for love to be returned– he loves loving just to give – the twinkle in his eye, the smile upon his face, when I fall down he picks me up with such amazing grace!"

. . . for being a hardworking farmer, brave soldier, true friend, incredible father and loving husband to my mother, Jean Friend.

Harold Eugene Friend
May 25, 1922 – May 4, 2009
War Hero – American Farmer – Father - Friend

R. FRIEND

Woolly Baaad Lies

Down on
Friendly Acres
#5

SUNFLOWER SEEDS PRESS

Dedication to Bill Ross

. . . thank you Bill Ross for your childlike creativity, your incredible imagination and your amazing illustrations that brought Friendly Acres to life. You will be missed as your artistic talents live on for years to come.

ISBN 9780983008903 Paperback
ISBN 9780983008910 Hardcover

Text copyright © 2011 "R. Friend" Ronda Friend
Illustrations by Doug Jones & Bill Ross
Graphic design by Julie Wanca Design

All rights reserved. Published by Sunflower Seeds Press, PO Box 1476, Franklin, Tennessee 37065

Library of Congress Control Number 2011920066

Printed in the U.S.A.
First Printing, Second printing - Sunflower Seeds Press

CONTENTS

The Friend Family

Duane, Ronda, Diane, and Ronald

CHAPTER 1

The Thingamabob

"*Fiddlesticks and gumdrop bars!* Help, someone, help! My hand's stuck and I can't get it out! There's a...a...a...**thingamabob** at the bottom of the bucket! Yikes!"

SQUAWK! SQUAWK! SQUAWK!

Hens dancin', wings flappin' 'n' feathers flyin', things were out of control! The more I screamed, the more the chickens squawked. I spotted Duane runnin' away from the chicken house with one hand coverin' what I believed was a big, fat grin. Then Duane disappeared. I knew it! My brother had somethin' to do with this, all right!

"Yikes! Ouch! Help!"

Finally, Momma heard my cry. Still wearin' her apron, she came runnin' into the chicken house. Tears trickled down my cheeks. "What's wrong, Ronda?"

"My hand is stuck and I can't get it loose. There's a thingamabob at the bottom of the bucket. I think my hand is broken!"

Elbow deep in chicken feed, Momma knelt down, cupped her hands and began scoopin' out the corn. After almost cryin' my eyes out, the pain suddenly disappeared. "I can't feel my hand anymore. It's numb and it's all Duane's fault—Mr. Cheesy *Pizza* himself!"

"Calm down, Ronda, and quit your glowering. We'll get to the bottom of this."

I have no idea what "glowerin'" is, I thought to myself. *And any hoot, I'm at the bottom and* that's the problem!

I couldn't look. Eyes tightly closed, I angrily murmured, "Momma, please get to the bottom and when you do, you'll realize this was *all* Duane's fault! My hand may be *numb,* but I'm not *dumb.* Duane had somethin' to do with this and I...I...I..."

"Oh me, oh my! Ronda, you need to be strong. This may hurt a little, but . . ."

"But what?"

"But it should be over in the blink of an eye!"

Momma freed my hand from the thingamabob.

"*Fiddlesticks and gumdrop bars!* It's broken, isn't it?" I wailed.

Little by little, the feelin' came back—and it wasn't a good one. My hand throbbed with pain to the point it was hard to catch my breath. Momma assured me that nothin' looked broken and I could open my eyes now. Wrapped in her arms with tears blurrin' my vision, I could tell my hand was red and swollen. I closed my eyes and recalled the "Chicken Fiasco." Diane, *Miss Hawkephant,* tattled...uh, I mean...told me all about it.

That's it! My hand looked just like Duane's when he came out of the chicken house, bawlin' like a baby with tears flowin' from his cheeks. Whimperin' like a puppy, Ronald followed, rubbin' his other set of *cheeks.* Daddy brought up the rear, luggin' two feed buckets. I pushed away from Momma, looked her square in the eyes and asked, "What was that . . .

thingamabob?"

Momma lifted the mysterious object in the air. I couldn't believe my eyes! "*This* was at the bottom of the bucket!" she declared. "And now *I'm* going to get to the bottom of this to find out *who* put it there!"

Mystery solved—a mouse trap! I bet I knew the rat that put it there and had an inklin' Momma knew too! I offered my expertise. "I'm a pretty good detective, like 'Dragnet,' so if you need help, just holler!"

Sufferin' from a strong urge to get back at my brother, my physical pain seemed to vanish. I opened the swingin' door with my good hand. Then I headed upstairs to *you-know-who's* room, chantin',

"Dum,'d dum, dum! Dum, 'd dum, dum dum!"

I think I smell a rat!

CHAPTER 2

Sisters Drive Their Brothers Mad!

You-know-who wasn't in his room. Hearin' a hullabaloo outside, I ran to my room, crawled up in my window seat and spied the culprit outside by the maple tree.

"Duane Hamilton Friend!!!"

You know what that spells—T-R-O-U-B-L-E! Today's my lucky day! I'm on the outside of trouble lookin' in for a change. My baby sister, Diane, isn't the only *Miss Hawkephant*. Hawk eyes focused and elephant ears positioned, I logged all the details.

"Young man," Momma instructed my brother, "wipe that glower off your face right now!"

There's that word again—*glower!*

"Your father and I can always count on you not to lie. But I can't understand for the life of me why you would turn around and do to Ronda what Ronald did to you."

"Momma, you don't understand," Duane pleaded. "You were an only child and you never had a baby brother or sister. Put yourself in my shoes. If you had a sister—especially one like Ronda—you'd realize that sometimes they can be a pain in the neck. They're not only buggy...they can pester you to no end!"

Unlike me, in front of crowds, Duane can be timid and shy. But when he's comfortable enough in front of someone, he'll take off talkin' to himself as though no one else is around. Momma had no control. Duane stood up, threw his hands in the air and pranced about in perfect rhythm, blurtin' out:

SISTERS – drive their brothers mad!

SISTERS – think brothers are bad!

SISTERS – rub some the wrong way!

SISTERS – get on nerves every day!

SISTERS – infuriate – frustrate!

SISTERS – rile, irk, aggravate!

SISTERS – drive you batty all day!

SISTERS – what more can I say?

"Nothing, Duane," Momma tried to interject. "You can stop right there....."

But Duane kept pluggin' away:

SISTERS – disturb – irritate!
SISTERS – annoy – agitate!
SISTERS – turn smiles into frowns!
SISTERS – wind you up – let you down!
SISTERS – make brother's blood boil!
SISTERS – most of them are spoiled!
SISTERS – not much I can do!
SISTERS – my luck – I've got two!

"Duane, I get it. Sometimes Ronda has the gift of getting on your nerves, but don't forget what Grandma Brombaugh always says, '*wait* and *think* before you act and do.' And take into account how much trouble Ronald got into. Didn't you learn anything from that?"

"I learned to *never, ever* under any circumstances use a *big muskrat trap* like Ronald did with me."

Mystery solved.

Curvin' both hands in a circle, Duane added, "When set, that trap is over six inches in diameter! I was in pain for days."

Evidently what *Miss Hawkephant* spied earlier was Ronald playin' the same trick on Duane. Only big brother used one of Daddy's humongous muskrat traps. Trappin' muskrats, raccoons and mink since he was only five years old, Daddy built up quite a business and even loaned money to his dad durin' the depression. In the *"Chicken Fiasco"* Ronald took Daddy's traps without permission—kind of like I did when I got into his tackle box. No wonder he got in so much trouble. Now where was I? Oh, yeah, I was eavesdroppin'.

"Momma, I need to be punished. But please, pretty please, keep in mind I decided *not* to use a *huge* trap. I didn't think a teeny, tiny one would hurt...much! Besides, it could have been worse. I thought of adding a mouse!"

Momma wasn't laughing.

"I really am sorry," he pleaded, soundin' like he really meant it for once. "What can I do to make it up to you and Ronda?"

"I want you to go help your father with a very smelly, nasty, disgusting job—hauling manure. Hopefully that will help you realize that the trick you pulled on your sister stunk too!"

Duane was gettin' off easy and notin' his expression, he thought so, too. My brother loves farm chores, so haulin' manure doesn't bother him one little bit! Besides, he'll just wear a bandana or clothespins on his nose to help with the smell.

Distracted by the honk of a car's horn, Duane turned to wave at Grandma pullin' into the driveway. Momma tapped him on the shoulder and added, "One more thing...Diane's going with me to the beauty parlor, so I need *you* to babysit Ronda this afternoon."

Duane is to babysit me? I'm *not* a baby!

My brother ran to the undercover angel for a much-needed hug. "Why so sad, Duane?" Grandma quizzed. "If I didn't know better, it looks like you're *glowering*!"

Duane explained his assignment. Playin' with his younger sister is *true* punishment. Duane looked devastated. I only smiled.

CHAPTER 3

Just a Teeny-Tiny Fib!

I bumpity-bumped on my bottom down the stairs and ran outside. Diane followed. Daddy arrived to help Grandma out of the car. When he picked up her knittin' basket out of the trunk, she grabbed it and handed it to me, informin' Daddy that he smelled so bad from haulin' manure that she didn't need his help.

Daddy put his hands on Duane's shoulders, "Son, it's time *you* get dirty!"

Grandma handed Diane some sheet music while she carried in her family's famous homemade German potato salad—Ronald's favorite! "What sweet angels you both are!"

Grandma, the *real* angel, noticed my red, swollen hand, so I caught her up on all the details. Eventually we ended up in the living room. I tried learnin' how to knit while Momma enjoyed her new music—"Rock Around the Clock!" Diane rocked so hard she fell right off her rocker!

After makin' sure Diane was all right, Momma asked me how my hand felt. I told her it was better. She assured me that she had taken care of the situation and that Duane was to babysit me later today. I told her I already knew. Startled, Momma questioned, "How did you know? Were you *eavesdropping*?"

The wrong answer just slipped out of my mouth before I could stop it. "No, it was just a lucky guess...I guess!"

Now why did I say that? Grandma lowered her knittin' needles and lifted her eyebrows over the top of her glasses. Had she seen me eavesdroppin' from my window? Momma went back to playin' the organ as I thought of ways to change the subject.

"Grandma, what does *glower* mean?"

Oops, why did I ask that? Grandma didn't flinch, but had me fetch the dictionary and read the definition. "Noah Webster's Dictionary says:

---

glower / glau˙(-ə)r / verb
2 : to look or stare with sullen annoyance or anger

"I knew it! I knew it!"

"Knew what?" Grandma asked.

"That was the look Duane gave...oh, never mind!"

My heart felt strange. Before I could change the subject again, Grandma reached for more yarn and let out a hoot 'n' a holler!

"HOOT! HOLLER!"

Frightened by the commotion, Diane screeched. Hawkephants do that. Momma simultaneously stepped on five pedals and mashed her hands on the keyboards. As she scooped Diane up in her arms to console her, she spied a thingamabob in Grandma's basket.

One wouldn't think an undercover angel would be scared to death of anything, but that thingamabob wasn't just anything. It was a mouse. And I had a hunch I knew the rat that put it there! Knowin' how deathly afraid of mice Grandma was, Momma let go of Diane and plucked it up. "Thank God, it's only a plastic mouse!" Momma exclaimed. "Mother, don't worry, I'll get to the bottom of this!"

Mommas do that a lot.

Grandma took a deep breath, closed her eyes, folded her hands and bowed her head. Adjustin' her halo...I mean her hat...she winked and said, "Prayer changes things. That was quite a surprise. Speaking of surprises, I have one in my purse for you girls!"

"Can I get it?"

"I know you 'can get it,' but you need permission. The proper way to ask is, 'May I get it?'"

"Oops! May I get it?"

"Yes, you may, and please bring the funnies from Sunday's papers while you're at it."

I headed to the back porch where Grandma always put her purse. There it was—Silly Putty, alongside some Chicklets. She always has gum. Tempted, yet focused, I ran back with the putty and the funnies. "Thanks, Grandma. Can I have some Chicklets too?"

"You can, but..."

Miss Hawkephant chimed in, *"May* I have thum?"

Sometimes Miss Hawkephant—the wannabe angel—can be so annoying! I corrected myself, "Oops! *May* I have some?"

"Yes, you *may* both count out fifteen pieces."

We raced to the back porch. Those itsy-bitsy pieces overflowed in Diane's teeny tiny palm. She plopped them into her mouth, countin', "Vun, two, free..."

I counted my fifteen Chicklets and noticed that my hand was bigger and able to handle more than fifteen. I popped the fifteen pieces in my mouth and remembered Grandma's exact words: "Count out fifteen pieces." But she never mentioned how many times. "Diane," I said, "run and thank Grandma."

Miss Hawkephant can't tattle now, I thought. Fifteen more pieces counted, I closed the packet, placed it neatly back into her purse and walked slowly while the gum *disappeared* in my mouth. I heard Diane exclaim, "Tanks for da Chickwets! You're tho thweet!"

Grandma smiled first at Diane. "I'm not as *thweet* as my granddaughters!" Her smile turned to a glower when she spotted *my* mouth. "Ronda, are you sure you took *fifteen* pieces?"

I said, "Yes," but really thought, *Twice,* then blurted out, "Fanks, Grandma!"

Diane laughed. Grandma didn't.

Did the undercover angel know? My heart poundin', I pretended like nothin' at all had happened, then grabbed the Silly Putty. Gently takin' it back, Grandma explained, "This putty is amazing. You can bounce it, break it and when you stretch it over an image, you can make an exact copy."

Grandma flattened it over our favorite comic strip, "Family Circle." After liftin' the putty off the comic strip, it copied right onto the Silly Putty. Grandma demonstrated. "Look, when you stretch the image, it starts to change the original picture. It reminds me of a situation when someone doesn't tell the truth. By telling a lie, the story stretches just a bit. Another lie stretches the truth a little more. When one tells more lies, eventually the image is distorted. I like Noah's explanation."

distort / dis-t ( ) rt / verb / 1 : to twist out of the
true meaning or proportion

image / 'im-ij / noun / 1 : a reproduction or imitation
of the form of a person or thing

My heart raced and my head hurt as Grandma
pulled the putty apart even more. "Girls, the more one
stretches the truth, the easier it becomes until too much
stretching turns a teeny-tiny white lie into a big, fat,
ugly lie, making it harder to tell what the truth was in
the first place."

Diane looked confused. I knew all too well *what*
Grandma was talkin' about and *who* she was talkin' to.
She concluded, "Thank God we each have a conscience.
Thank God for Noah and his definitions."

conscience / kän-ch n(t)s / noun / 1 : the sense . . . of
the moral goodness . . . of one's own conduct,
intention or character together with a feeling of
obligation to do right or be good

CHAPTER 4

Pullin' the Wool Over Your Eyes

When it was almost time for lunch, Grandma asked us girls for our ABC gum. Diane started recitin' her ABC's as I explained that ABC gum just meant gum that has *Already Been Chewed*. Instantly, Diane stuck her tongue out for Grandma to take her wad. In a pickle, I quickly slipped my piece into her Kleenex. The undercover angel appeared not to be surprised. Did she notice how much bigger my wad was than Diane's? I hoped not.

Momma was fixin' Daddy's favorite sandwich— the "Dagwood." Before my parents dated, she worked as a waitress at the only drive-in restaurant for miles— "The Toot." The most popular items on the menu were Dagwood sandwiches (thirty-five cents) and a Black Cow, which was ice cream covered with root beer (ten cents).

"The Toot" was named The Toot because a drive-up customer would have to *toot* his horn as a signal, lettin' the waitress know he was ready to order. At The Toot, Daddy would wait to *toot* to make sure that when he did *toot*, Momma was the waitress ready to answer the *toot*. "Goo-goo eyes" glazin', he'd order a Dagwood and a Black Cow.

To make a Dagwood, Momma started with a fried hamburger and a slice of cheese on top of a piece of toast. Grandma pressed her hamburger in between a towel, which squeezed out all the grease. On top of the cheeseburger, Momma added relish, mayonnaise and a slice of onion, then another piece of toast. The second layer consisted of bacon, lettuce 'n' tomato, plus another piece of toast. Carefully insertin' two toothpicks in opposite corners, she pressed down and then cut the tall sandwich diagonally in half.

Bacon sizzlin' in the skillet, plus a mound of it drainin' on a paper towel, was all it took to make my mouth water. *I was starved.* Momma told me to fetch the can of lard for the bacon grease. My stomach growled like a bear comin' out of hibernation. No one appeared to be lookin', so I snatched two pieces of bacon, then headed to the back porch.

Bacon safely stashed in my stomach, my hunger pains disappeared, but my heart was achin' and I felt warm all over. Returnin' with the lard can, I smelled something awful and nasty.

The boys had opened the back door. That's all it took for the manure smell to spread and stink. Daddy popped his head in the kitchen, gave Momma some goo-goo eyes and even added a *smink*. That's what Daddy calls a smile and a wink combined—a *smink*! The *smink* didn't stop Momma from directin' them down to the basement for a shower and a change of clothes.

Farmers can get downright filthy dirty. With only one bathtub upstairs, Daddy put a shower in the basement. There's nothing schmancy fancy about it—not even a curtain. Momma makes us wear thongs on our feet even though we stand on a wood slat so the water drains well.

Grandma shook her head, placed her potato salad on the table and commented, "No matter how fast they hurry downstairs, the manure odor seems to linger. It stinks, doesn't it, Ronda? It's hard to cover up something so nasty."

Grandma wasn't just talkin' about manure. So, was she thinkin' about my fib—knowin' Duane's punishment—or the teeny-tiny lie about the Chicklets, or had she seen me sneak the bacon? I tried to act as though nothin' had happened, so one-handed, (my other hand still recoverin' from the mouse trap) I helped set the table.

Showers completed and half of the Dagwoods made, we all sat down and bowed our heads. Diane shut her eyes so tight her face was twisted—cute, but distorted. Everyone had one eye open, watchin' as she prayed: "Gawd is gwate, Gawd is good, and we fank Him for our food. By His hands we all are fed, fank You, Gawd, for daywee bwed. AMEN!"

She watched as we clapped. "That's my little angel," Daddy boasted.

As the baby in the family, Diane gets a lot of attention, but even I hafta admit that she's adorable—maybe not always an angel—but adorable.

Grandma got up to finish the rest of the sandwiches. "Jean, there's not enough bacon left for both sandwiches."

My body sat motionless while my eyeballs were on a roll. No one noticed me lookin' around except the undercover angel. I knew it. Grandma knew what I knew. I'd hogged the bacon! I can't put anything past her. I bet she knows about the Chicklets too!

"Really," Momma replied, "I thought for sure I'd fried enough bacon."

"Somebody must have been achin' for some bacon," joked Daddy. "Who snitched some pieces?"

Everyone simultaneously blurted out, "Not me!"—except *me*. My "Not me!" came out last and loudest. Now I knew that sayin', "Not me!" was wrong, but I also knew that if I now said, "Me!" I would get in trouble and possibly be sent to my room *without* lunch. It seemed the more fibs I told, the easier it was to tell a few more. Besides, I was hungry.

"We probably counted wrong." Grandma responded, "We'll just share the last piece."

Everyone noticed that the last piece was very small. My once empty stomach began to ache again. Those teeny-tiny lies were takin' their toll. I felt awful, but tried my best not to let it show.

Diane was ecstatic, sharin' about our new Silly Putty. That's all it took for *Mr. World Bookworm Encyclopedia*. Ronald took off! "Did you know Silly Putty was accidentally invented during WW II? The rubber-producing countries in the Far East were destroyed, which kept America from producing much-needed tires and boots. James Wright, a Scottish engineer, produced a gooey substance which, when rolled into a ball, bounced higher than any ball he'd ever seen. Scientists tried to find a practical use, but failed."

Since Ronald was hoggin' the whole conversation, Chatty Cathy wouldn't have been able to get a word in edgewise. Ronald's not a big talker unless he's read about somethin', especially in the *World Book*.

"However," he went on—he wasn't about to stop now— "Peter Hodgson, $14,000 in debt, had faith in Silly Putty's potential. Borrowing $147, he introduced it at the 1950 International Toy Fair in New York. Utilizing an old barn as a warehouse, he began distributing Silly Putty in used egg cartons to stores like Neiman-Marcus and Doubleday bookstores."

Appearin' not to take a breath, Ronald rambled on, "A New York writer discovered Silly Putty and wrote an article. Three days after the magazine was released, Mr. Hodgson received a quarter million orders for his product."

"Ronald, what a wonderful lesson on ingenuity," Grandma politely interrupted. "A 'mistake' turned into an incredible surprise and an awesome business venture!"

"Speaking of business," Daddy added, "boys, you're going to have your hands full shearin' sheep today."

That's all it took for *Mr. Know-It-All* to blurt out everythin' he knows about sheep—and then some. "It's amazing! Once the wool is off, the imperfections lying beneath the wool are exposed. Those imperfections had been covered up with layer upon layer of wool!"

"You're not trying to 'pull the wool over our eyes,' are you?" joked Daddy.

Ignorin' the question, Ronald kept going: "In the 1900s, men in Europe wore wigs made of wool in the British court. Some still do today."

"Ronald," Daddy jumped in, "you'd better eat. By pulling that bright, white, woolly wig down over a person's eyes, one couldn't see what was really happening. So if a clever lawyer fooled the judge, he was said to be 'pulling the wool' over his eyes. He'd do anything, including cheating, stretching the truth or even lying to make that happen."

My stomach churned. The undercover angel added, "The more lies told, the more lies were needed to cover up the first lies in the first place. By the way, which one of you tried to 'pull the wool over my eyes' this morning?"

Was she lookin' at me? *My heart stopped*. Was she *talkin'* about me? *I felt hot*. No one responded. Grandma clarified, "The rubber mouse?"

I sighed in relief as the boys shook their heads no. Momma glanced at Daddy, "Harold Eugene Friend, I always know when you're covering up something. I can see it in your eyes! It was you, wasn't it?"

"My lies have been exposed," Daddy pleaded guilty, "I can *never* pull the wool over Momma's eyes!"

"Phooey, Harold. It was a good thing it wasn't real. I should have known you were up to your old tricks."

"I'm shocked, Edna. You've always been able to smell a *rat* a mile away," Daddy added, battin' his eyes and grinnin'. "Sorry, Grandma, that was *cheesy*!"

"Harold," Momma pleaded, "take that *sheepish* grin off your face!"

"Sorry...I've been *baaaaaad!*"

"*Woolly baaaaad*," Diane added.

Everybody baaaad.

"Speaking of sheep, Ronald, you've outdone yourself with the shears we bought," Daddy bragged. "Grandma Friend would be so proud."

"It took us months to save up enough money to buy them since they were $60," Momma added. "And to think, Ronald, Daddy doesn't even have to help you anymore."

"That's because he has *me*," boasted Duane.

Grandma Friend loved sheep. One of Daddy's favorite pictures—of a farmer plowin' the fields with his wife tendin' their flock—hung in her parlor. It's in Ronald's room now.

Now, where was I? Oh, yeah, Ronald once again took over the table talk. "I've promised to pay for those shears. The going rate for one sheep's wool is $1.25. By my calculations, I'll need to shear 48 sheep to pay..."

"...and that's what happens when the wool gets to the market," Ronald concluded...finally!

I must have zoned out for a minute or so. Daddy asked if anything was wrong. When I don't talk, everybody thinks I'm sick. I told him I was fine...just great...*another lie.*

"Boys, before you start shearing, Duane has a special job to do. Ronald, you can help me pull weeds in the garden. Remember, if it weren't for farmers..."

"We'd all be hungry and naked," everyone chimed in.

CHAPTER 5

Wild Idea

It was almost time for Duane's punishment— *babysittin' me*. I skipped into the kitchen, holdin' onto Momma's favorite children's book, *Animals of the Bible*, just in time to hear her babysittin' instructions: "Duane, be good and play with your sister. I'll be home around two-thirty. And, Ronda, be sure to listen to your brother."

"Yes, Momma!"

We watched as Grandma, Momma and Diane piled into Grandma's green Chevrolet coupe. Daddy and Ronald waved good-bye from the garden.

"Duane, I have a wild idea. Let's pretend we're artists just like Dorothy Lanthrop in her book, *Animals of the Bible*. She carefully carted animals into her house, perfectly positioned them and voila — a work of art!"

Duane didn't seem thrilled, but I begged 'n' begged. "Momma wouldn't care. It was her *favorite* book. Besides, you're supposed to play with me."

Reluctantly he helped collect an easel, paint, paintbrushes and a sketch pad from the play closet. The Swiss cuckoo clock struck one. We had almost two hours to create our masterpiece.

The setup in the parlor was picture-perfect. There was only one thing missing — music. So, before collectin' our critters, I grabbed one of my favorite forty-five speed, turntable records — "Hokey Pokey" on one side; "The Bunny Hop" on the other. I inserted the yellow plastic disk into the record, which I placed on the turntable, and presto — music.

"The Bunny Hop" was released in 1952 — three years before I was born. Momma tells me I'd hop inside her tummy every time it played. Music blarin', Duane hopped around, drapin' an ottoman with an old sheet. Obviously, he'd warmed up to my wild idea.

When it was time to assemble our masterpiece, entitled, "The Animals of Friendly Acres," my first stop was Diane's baby bunnies. Since the garage was in between the garden and their pens, it would be easy to sneak them inside without havin' to explain things to Daddy.

Moments later — mission accomplished. I released those adorable bunnies from their cage and instantly they boogied down to "The Bunny Hop." Duane rushed out of the room, only to reappear with some newspapers just in case the bunnies left some *you-know-what* on the floor.

I gave Duane the thumbs-up, grabbed an old shoebox, rushed out to the chicken house (once again, out of sight from the garden) and hand-picked a trio of baby chicks. When I returned, I noticed that my brother had closed the parlor doors, the outside door and the swingin' door that led to my parents' bedroom. We'd have no problems keepin' our art critters under control.

Lovin' their new hangout, the bouncin' baby bunnies welcomed the babblin' baby birds. Only one slight problem—we were havin' just a little trouble keepin' them in one place. Whisperin' another idea in Duane's ear, he responded, "You don't think Momma will get mad, do you?"

"No way, Duane. Remember, the book was the first Caldecott children's picture book award winner. And don't forget—Momma's favorite!"

"Okay, but if she gets mad, *you* will have to tell the truth. This whole wacky, wild idea was *yours* in the first place. Scram! I'll hold down the fort."

After grabbin' my hooded sweatshirt with the big sewn-in front pocket, I skedaddled. My next destination was harder to accomplish than I imagined. When I passed by the garden, I told Daddy that I was fetchin' somethin' I'd forgotten from the shed. He waved and gave the thumbs-up. (Okay, I stretched the truth a little, but I was gettin' somethin'!)

Once little stinkers hear humans, they can't stop squealin'. Deafenin' to my ears, the feeder doors slapped back 'n' forth as the sows snorted and the little ones sniffed for slop. I grabbed two plump porkers, placed them in my front pocket and darted toward the house. With my sweatshirt squirmin' 'n' squealin' up a storm, would it be possible to sneak past the gardeners without them noticin'? Fortunately, Daddy started up the rototiller about that time. They didn't even look in my direction.

Safely inside, I encountered chirpin' chicks, bouncin' bunnies and Duane dancin' around on his knees, spreadin' some more newspaper. One never knows *when, where* or *if* our farm friends might decide to *you-know-what*. Good thing the parlor had wooden floors.

Duane grabbed the playful piggies, then posed and propped them up as I rearranged the bunnies and chicks. Everything seemed picture perfect.

All smiles, Duane darted out the front door. Returnin' moments later with a saggin' sack swaddled in his arms, he grinned. "Grandma Friend would *love* this!"

Duane tried handin' over the bulgin' burlap bag to me, but the sack began to wiggle 'n' waggle uncontrollably. Duane howled, *"Help me, Ronda. Help, help me, Ronda!"*

There he goes again with that great song idea. *"Help me, Ronda. Help, help me, Ronda!"* There's no time for that right now!

Together we took control. Duane reached inside the bag and pulled out a precious little lamb complete with some straw. The lamb seemed to have a calmin' effect on all the other critters, or was it "The Bunny Hop" playin' softly in the background? Whatever it was, everythin' was runnin' like clockwork. We scattered the straw and laid the bag aside.

Now our precious portrait really did seem picture-perfect! Pretendin' to be our family photographer, Mr. Priser, I grabbed my Bozo, the Clown and softly crooned,

"Gitchie-gitchie-goo! Smile! Gitchie-gitchie-goo!"

This was a piece of cake. Subjects smilin', we were ready to create our masterpiece. As we turned to pick up our paintbrushes, however, the *empty* burlap bag bobbled across the floor!

Oh, rats! Actually, it was a *mouse* that triggered pandemonium. The next few minutes overflowed with chaos, confusion and bedlam all rolled into one! Our piece of cake was startin' to **crumble!**

Crash, Boom, Bang!

The parlor turned into a three-ring circus, clown included. Music still playin', the bunnies hopped right off the ottoman, the chicks flapped their wings and tried to fly, but fell to the floor in a split position; the lamb frolicked frantically around the room, while the piggies snorted and burrowed themselves under the burlap bag. Newspapers, paint, brushes and even Bozo went airborne!

The mouse went up the clock, which was about to strike two—oh, no, *two o'clock*!

"Duane, this is an emergency!" Hands raised in the air, I repeated, "*This is an emergency*!"

"*Cheesy pizza*, Ronda, remember this was *your* wild and wacky idea—your brainstorm! But if you ask me, it's more like a tornado!"

Together we caged the bunnies, boxed the chickens, pocketed the piggies and bundled the lamb in burlap. Worn out and totally exhausted, we *wee weeed* the plump piggies and their newfound friends *all* the way home—*their* homes, that is!

Returnin' to the parlor, we worked nonstop cleanin' up paint, newspapers and *you-know-what*. With fifteen minutes to spare, it seemed our tracks were covered. "Duane, what are we gonna tell Momma?"

"You mean what are *you* gonna tell Momma! It was *your* fault!"

Exhausted, we plopped down on the couch and checked off our list. Bunnies—check. Chicks—check. Lamb and piggies—check. Paint supplies—check. Had we forgotten anything?

Fiddlesticks and gumdrop bars! The light bulb went off simultaneously in our heads. Everythin' was in order except one *thingamabob*—a mouse was still in the house, and it wasn't a rubber one. And with Grandma scared to death of mice, time was runnin' out! Down on our knees and in desperation, we began our search.

"Here, mousey, mousey! Here, mousey, mousey."

"*Cheesy pizza*, Ronda, do you *really* expect the mouse to come to you? We don't have time to spare!" Duane yelled as he ran out of the house.

Duane returned. Why hadn't I thought of this? In his arms was Snowball, our barn cat. The molasses was almost totally gone from her previous fiasco. Taggin' alongside were Teeny and Tiny, our *rat* terriers. My brother had the perfect plan except for one *minor* detail—Momma and Grandma *never ever* allow dogs or cats in the house. But this was *an emergency!*

No time to lose, the trio began their mad search to be the first one to catch our uninvited guest. We joined the hunt. On all fours and on the floor, we scoured the parlor. The mouse could have easily slipped under doors, so Duane instructed me to go through the living room while he searched our parents' bedroom. We'd meet in the kitchen. Great idea!

Focused and still on all fours, we met in the kitchen. Only one problem—**one BIG problem**—we detected three pairs of legs: one teeny-tiny pair of legs, one pair of legs with pedal pushers and one pair of legs wearin' hose with a white slip showin'.

Oh, no! The trio's back!

Slowly raisin' our heads, we first spotted Diane. We looked higher and discovered Momma and Grandma glowerin' at both of us! The undercover angel spoke first, "Tish, tish, tish! This gets my goat!"

There aren't many things that get Grandma's goat, but I told you a dog or a cat in this house is one of 'em.

"Take those animals *outside* and then meet me *inside* immediately," Momma ordered.

"But, Momma, there's a..."

"No ifs, ands or buts—just do as I say! *But* both of you can rest assured I *am* going to get to the *bottom* of this!"

Stinky, Smelly Lies!

Fortunately pets come when you call their names. It didn't take any time at all to get Snowball, Teeny and Tiny outside. We were discouraged that our masterpiece had fallen apart. And where in the world was the *you-know-what*? Duane and I reluctantly headed inside. Momma and Grandma were sniffin' and chorusin', "P.U.! What's that smell?"

"*Fiddlesticks and gumdrop bars!*" I gasped.

"I'm pretty sure *it isn't* fiddlesticks and gumdrop bars," Momma responded, "Duane! Ronda! Follow me!"

We all ended up in the parlor (even Miss Hawkephant). I was puzzled. We had cleaned up after the animals, spilled paint, brushes and even the rolled-up newspapers. But evidently we'd missed some *stinky, smelly you-know-what!* Grandma pointed to a few little black pellets on the floor behind the couch. We had been

"What happened?" Momma's interrogation began. "Whose *wild idea* was this anyway?"

"What do you mean?"

"Ronda, you know *exactly* what I mean. But I'd like to hear Duane's story first since he was in charge."

Great! Duane almost never lies. He can't stand *not* tellin' the truth. And when he worries too much, *you-know-what* happens! He breaks out in hives. Both pointer fingers aimed my way, Duane shouted, "It was Ronda's *wild idea*—*she* made me do it!"

"Oh, yeah?"

"Uh, huh!"

"Oh, yeah?"

"Uh, huh!"

"Oh, yeah?"

"Uh, huh!"

Furious, Duane shouted, "*Liar, liar, pants on fire!*"

"That's it! Stop, right this instant," Momma commanded. "Each of you has some explaining to do."

Feelin' hot, I looked down to make sure my pants weren't on fire. They weren't. Momma sent Diane upstairs for her nap. Although I knew better, Miss Hawkephant would be listenin' in instead of sleepin'. Meanwhile, Duane gave me the eye, and it wasn't *goo-goo* ones. It was more like *cuckoo-cuckoo* eyes, and I was the *cuckoo*!

Grandma kept Duane in the parlor. Momma took me to the kitchen. Scared, I had no idea what Duane's story was gonna be. Maybe this time Duane wouldn't tell the truth. No one is perfect *all* the time.

I couldn't believe what my tongue started sayin'. I blurted out that it was all Duane's wild idea and that I'd warned my brother not to, but he did it anyway. Momma asked if I had told her the whole truth and nothin' but the truth. My heart poundin', I declared boldly, "Yes, Momma, I've told the truth—nothin' but the truth!"

Now what made me say that? I didn't tell the truth at all. I couldn't believe what had just come out of my mouth. What was I thinkin'? I guess I wasn't. I can't keep pullin' the wool over Momma's eyes. I needed to tell the truth. I heard commotion.

HOOT!!! HOLLER!!!

"*It's an emergency!*" Grandma shouted. "Jean, grab a broom!"

Broom in hand, Momma ran to the rescue. I followed. Grandma was standin' on top of the ottoman, screamin' at the top of her lungs. I was shocked. Her rule is to *never, ever* stand on furniture! I guess this really *was* an emergency!

Duane held the door open to the outside as all mayhem broke loose. Grandma, not much of a dancer, was jivin' 'n' a jiggin' to beat the band. Momma swatted furiously with her broom every which way until the mouse, just as frightened as Grandma, left the house!

Pandemonium over, Grandma and Momma calmed down. Whisperin,' they appeared to be comparin' notes. Duane and I sat motionless at opposite ends of the couch. He appeared *calm, cool and collected.* I was *tense, twitchy and troubled.* By the expression on Momma's face, I could tell our stories didn't match.

My eyes shifted down. Momma instructed me to look up straight into her eyeballs. She believed it made you listen and understand better—like lookin' into someone's heart. Out of the corner of my eye, I noticed Duane was starin' straight into her eyes. I feared she saw the lies in my eyes.

Although proud of Duane's truthfulness, Momma explained that he had been left in charge and had used poor judgment. Understandin' we were just tryin' to have fun, Momma said if we had only asked permission, she would have helped us set up everything in the back room of the chicken house, where the lambs are born in the winter. We could have had all the fun we wanted. But when we brought animals into the house— that was another story!

For usin' poor judgment, Duane was sent off to haul manure *again*. My consequences were much different. I was in

D-O-u-B-L-E
T-R-O-U-B-L-E !

Momma explained, "I'm disappointed in both of you. I believe Duane told me the truth. I believe you didn't, Ronda. I could see it in your eyes. You need some time to think."

I went to my time-out chair *again!*

CHAPTER 7

Buggy Brothers!

Brothers can be *so* buggy! One moment we're havin' fun, and the next, we're at each other's throats. Oh well, Grandma Brombaugh always says, "When life gives you lemons—make lemonade!" It's time-out again, so time to make lemonade. I'll write a song! This one is dedicated to *you-know-who*.

Brothers, Brothers

Creepy, crawly, buggy-wuggie brothers!
Never do they listen to a word we say –
they tend to rub us the wrong way!
Aggravate – frustrate – every little thing
that girls are doing.
When our brothers show up, you'll all agree:
Boys are as annoying as a skinned-up knee!

All kinds of problems, they become a nuisance,
like a fly on your apple pie!
Painful like a crick in the neck, look at us –
we're such a wreck!
They pester, agitate for fun! Uh-huh!

Those who – know us – realize that we love to
cause a big fuss!
Parents always know that's how
siblings show their love.

53

Lord, help us sisters
to not give our brothers a blister!
And, Lord, help our brothers
realize sisters grow up to be moms!

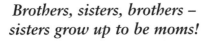

Brothers, sisters, brothers –
sisters grow up to be moms!

Fiddlesticks and gumdrop bars! With that off my chest, I was totally determined to think things through. I thought 'n' I thought 'n' I thought! I thought so much I thought I heard a tiny voice inside my head. Could it be *my conscience?* I closed my eyes real tight to concentrate and heard it again.

When I opened my eyes, I couldn't believe it. Sittin' on top of my bed was a very tall, slender, yet—comparatively speakin'—teeny-tiny bug with a pair of huge glasses sittin' cockeyed on his nose, coverin' up the bluest eyes ever. Could it really be my *conscience?* Looked more like a *bug* to me!

The bug talked. It asked me if I knew my mouth was wide open. In somewhat of a *buggy voice* it continued, "It's not a good habit to get into for a variety of reasons—always keeping your mouth open, that is. Sometimes humans can talk 'n' talk just to hear themselves talk; therefore, never listening to others or, if their mouth is continuously open, he or she can catch *a cold or a bug or a falling star or something!*"

I shut my mouth, cupped my hands to my cheeks and stared. It continued, "Let me introduce myself. My name is *Billy Bob, the Bed Bug*. I realize that you don't believe in bed bugs. I wouldn't either if I were you—*but I do*. I exist—therefore, I believe. I'm alive and *ticking*! Pardon the *bug* pun!"

It took a breath, so I asked, "Why are you here?"

"Sent from above, I'm at your service. I believe there are several things today that have been, shall we say, *bugging* you today and that they are all centered around one thing. I wish there was a better way of putting this, but the word is *lying*, which comes from the word *lie*. I like Noah's definition best:

Lie / 'l / verb / 1 : to make an untrue
statement with the intent to deceive;
an intentional untruth; a falsehood.
2 : to create a false or misleading impression

He knows Noah! I was speechless; the bug wasn't.

"I've been sent from on high to be by your side and remind you of wise things to do—like when your tongue is tied and you're petrified, you're tempted to tell lies, then shut your eyes, raise your battle cry, be strong and tell the truth. Excuse me, my friend, my new friend—I mean, R. Friend—your mouth is wide open *again*."

"That's because I'm *tryin'* to tell you somethin'!"

"Forgive me."

56

"Thank you. Ahem! Well, *Mr. Blue-eyed Billy Bob, the Bed Bug*, my daddy says there are no such things as bed bugs anymore. Besides, I sleep on a mattress and box springs."

"*Bugjuice*! I'm a bed bug—a harmless bed bug. I'm telling you the truth. There's one thing you'll *never, ever* catch a bed bug in—that would be a lie! We always tell the truth. I may be just a *teeny-tiny, teensy-weensy, minute, microscopic, miniscule bed bug* – but I'll never, ever tell a white lie, a big fat lie, or any other kind of lie, for that matter."

"You've *never, ever* lied in your whole life?"

"Never, ever—*cross my antennae—hope to fly— stick a beetle in my eye*. The Bed Bug Motto is simply: '*We don't fly and we don't lie!*'"

"That's incredible! You are one special, extraordinary, remarkable bug. Tell me your secret."

I reached out to touch him, but Billy Bob, the Bed Bug disappeared. In the blink of a blue-eyed bug's eye, he was gone!

Just then Momma popped her head in my room, informin' me that time was up and then asked if I had anything to say. Tongue-tied, I wanted to confess, but I was petrified. I told her my mind was full and, when it cleared up, I'd be able to talk. (Besides, I was still wonderin' if I really do just talk to hear myself talk.) Momma reminded me that this incident wasn't over and for the second part of my punishment, I was to haul manure.

I was sure of one thing:

manure stinks.

It's hard to maneuver in manure. Some deep sections all but covered my rubber boots. Several times I got stuck. Daddy was always there to rescue me. Exhausted from pullin' me out of the manure, he finally sent Duane and me outside to the cattle lot to scrape and gather dried manure into burlap feed sacks. It works great in the garden as fertilizer to make the plants grow. At least, manure is good for somethin'! Finished, we raced to see who could take their shower first.

I lost!

CHAPTER 8

Squeaky Clean!

Duane, squeaky clean from his shower, informed me that there was no more hot water. Since I was spendin' the night with Grandma, she insisted that I take my bath at her house, so we could go on home before dark. Duane insisted on gettin' my overnight bag that I had packed earlier in the day.

Filthy dirty, I sat on a towel in the backseat of the car. Grandma likes things squeaky clean, so her house fits her to a tee—clean, white, small and pleasant! She didn't want my smelly, stinky clothes in her house, either, so when we arrived, I stayed on the back porch while Grandma took things inside.

Her house doesn't have a bathtub or a shower. It was only a few years ago that Grandma got indoor plumbing. Off her *itsy-bitsy bedroom* is an even smaller *itsy-bitsy bathroom* with only a sink and a toilet. Before that, everyone did their duties in her outhouse. I remember that bein' *really stinky*!

Grandma returned to help pump the water for my bath. The big green pump was almost as tall as me. Together we held onto the huge handle and pumped up 'n' down, up 'n' down, up 'n' down. Grandma called that *primin' the pump*. Just when you thought nothin' was about to happen, water flowed out of the pump into the bucket.

Water heatin' up on the stove, Grandma placed a big gray galvanized tub on the kitchen floor. After fillin' the tub with a combination of hot 'n' cold water, she lathered up her homemade soap while I undressed on the back porch. Her house was elevated off the ground, and Grandma assured me that the neighbors could not see through the windows. But just in case, I always ran 'n' plopped into the tub of hot, sudsy water before you could say, "*Fiddlesticks and gumdrop bars!*"

Guidelines for bathin' were posted on the wall next to me. I reminded Grandma that I wasn't a baby anymore. She whispered, "I'll leave you alone, but remember, you'll always be my baby! Besides if you follow the order, you'll be *squeaky clean!*"

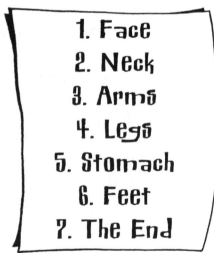

1. Face
2. Neck
3. Arms
4. Legs
5. Stomach
6. Feet
7. The End

Hee! Hee!

That note always makes me chuckle!

Grandma went to the living room for her usual routine of pullin' out the sleeper sofa, makin' my bed, and grabbin' my pjs from the overnight bag. Only this time I heard a loud ruckus!

SCREAM!!!

I bolted straight out of the tub, but realizin' the neighbors might see, I plopped right back down. The screamin' stopped. My overnight bag in one hand and a plastic mouse in the other, Grandma appeared in the doorway with an expression on her face that made me think *she* thought it was *my* idea.

"I didn't have anythin' to do with it, Grandma! Honest, I didn't."

Grandma, still a bit skeptical, sat down at the kitchen table to catch her breath. *Now* I knew why Duane *insisted* on gettin' my bag.

"Are you sure you're telling the truth *this time?*"

I hesitated to respond. Besides, she would never believe me now. Tryin' to muster up enough courage to tell the truth, I inquired, "Grandma, did you ever lie when you were little?"

"I did." She sighed. "We all make mistakes. There are times we think lying will get us out of a sticky situation. But the truth is, the truth is eventually uncovered one way or the other. The best thing to do is tell the truth right from the start."

"What happened to make you stop tellin' lies?"

"When I was about your age, Mother and I made a huge batch of potato salad for a church picnic. A huge chunk disappeared from the middle of the bowl. *I was hungry.*"

Thinkin' about the bacon, I replied, "*Really hungry?*"

"My stomach was *growling like a bear coming out of hibernation.* When Mother asked if I had been in the potato salad, my brain said *yes* and my lips said *no. I knew Mother knew.* But I didn't have enough courage to confess. A half-hour later, she sent me to fetch more potatoes down in the dark cellar. I was scared to death of what I found there."

"What was it?"

"Staring right at me was a beady-eyed dead mouse. And that wasn't all. The mouse was sitting smack-dab on a stinky, shriveled-up potato. The potato had been in the dark so long that it had lanky, tangled roots sticking out of its eyes. That *distorted image* still gives me the *heebie-jeebies.* To this day, I think Mother put it there so I could learn my lesson.

"Ronda, it was so *nasty*! Mother told me that lies are nasty and that lies try to cover up the truth, but what really happens is that one small lie just leads to many more lies until we find ourselves not only in the dark, but in a *tangled mess.*

"Mother shared that humans, mice and potatoes have one thing in common—eyes! By looking deep into a person's eyes, one can discern if that person is *telling the truth* or not. I confessed right then and there. 'Mother, I ate the potato salad.' She admitted she already knew. From that point on, I was afraid of two things: *not telling the truth* and..."

"*Mice!*"

"How did you know?"

"Lucky guess!"

"My guess is your bath water is cold and I need to take my sponge bath." Leavin', she added, "Besides, it looks like you're *squeaky clean* on the outside."

Squeaky clean on the outside, I thought, *but not so squeaky clean on the* inside.

Ready for bed, I heard the television. *Fiddlesticks and gumdrop bars! Grandma's lettin' me watch a half-hour show before bedtime!* Lo 'n' behold, the program that was on was "To Tell the Truth!" I turned off the TV and began to mull over the day's events. I thought 'n' I thought 'n' I thought.

Oh no, not again! He's back! Makin' sure Grandma wasn't nearby, I whispered, "Billy Bob, the Bed Bug, what are *you* doin' here?"

"Now that's a *buggy* question—a human asking why a bed bug is on a bed! The simple answer: *It's a bed!* It's where I call home. And to tell the whole truth and nothing but the truth—I found my way here via your overnight bag. Remember, I don't fly. Now for my question to you: Did you tell *you-know-who you-know-what*?"

"Tell who what?"

"Tell the undercover angel the truth yet?"

"No, I'm afraid to! I wish I could have the *courage* to be more like you!"

"Oh, you don't want to be like me. I might never ever tell a lie—but look at me. If I only had a personality, I could be somebody! But as it is, I'm just a bug—just a *measly, scrawny, insignificant insect—a puny, pathetic parasite.*"

"Billy Bob, the Bed Bug, I don't think you're a puny, pathetic parasite. Grandma Brombaugh would say, '*Hogwash! Billy Bob, the Bed Bug, you have potential!*'"

"Bugjuice! I'm telling you the truth. I'm basically *a mess*—except remember, I don't lie! You *really* think I have potential?"

"*Potential and possibilities.* I promise, with a little confidence, you can become an *incredible insect, the perfect pest, the best bug, and an out-of-the-ordinary, one-of-a-kind, creepin', crawlin' critter*! All you need is a little confidence, and I can help you with that later. But right now, I need *you* to help *me.* Today I started out tellin' just a few little lies. I continued with a few more lies, which only got me deeper 'n' deeper in trouble—so deep I don't know if I can get out of this mess. All I know is I *hafta*!"

"Ronda, the best thing to do is to tell the truth from the get-go. You've dug yourself into a deep hole. The only way out now is to *confess* your lies. Now I can't tell the truth for you, but I can be your friend, your cheerleader and your confidant. If I *hafta,* I'll bug you enough until you *hafta* tell the truth!"

"Now that's a true friend."

Billy Bob smiled. "Gotta *flee*!"

And he did.

"Ronda, did you say something? I'll be right there!"

I know what you're thinkin'. All ready for bed, Grandma will appear in her cute little blue nightie 'n' slippers with *no hat,* therefore unveilin' her *halo.* I'm not tryin' *to pull the wool over your eyes,* but you'll *never, ever* see Grandma's halo. But don't take my word for it. Grandma always told us, "*A picture is worth a thousand words!*"

I told you! Grandma might look silly, but ladies these days spend a lot of money (three dollars) gettin' their hair teased 'n' sprayed with tons of hairspray. They aren't about to go to bed, then wake up with *bed head*. So at night, with the help of a whole roll of toilet paper, a black net and a few bobby pins, women wrap their doos. Next mornin' after removin' the pins and net, they carefully undo the toilet paper, then fold it in order to reuse it the next night. Their beautiful, bouffant hairdos are intact—not even one hair out of place! Now, where was I?

Oh, yeah. Grandma sat down on my bed and asked me if "To Tell the Truth" was a good one. After no response, she softly spoke, "Do you have something you need to get off your chest?"

She knows my chest hurts! I *hafta* tell the truth! I sat up, stared straight into her eyes, then blurted out in one breath, "Earlier, I was afraid to confess but I've told a couple lies—maybe even more than a couple. Today, while wallowin' in the manure, I realized the deeper my boots went in *you-know-what*, the harder it was to get out. Just like the more lies I told kept gettin' me deeper 'n' deeper 'n' deeper in trouble. It seemed the more lies I told, the harder it was to get out of them. So here goes: I lied about the Chicklets and took fifteen pieces—*twice*."

I felt soooooo much better!

Like a bolt from the blue, I eyed Billy Bob, the Bed Bug, jumpin' up 'n' down, cheerin'!

"I lied about the bacon. I guess you could say, 'I was *achin' for some bacon* and ate the *missing pieces.*'"

Billy Bob, the Bed Bug, did a somersault.

"I lied about the animals in the house. It was *totally* my idea, not Duane's."

Billy Bob, the Bed Bug, did a back flip.

"I told so many lies today that tomorrow I promise to tell Momma the truth."

Grandma grabbed a small ball of Silly Putty and bounced it on the floor, and it went every which way. "Your lies have been bouncing off the wall today. Lies on top of lies cause chaos and confusion. *Remember, lies stretch and grow then in a blink, start to spread, smell, swell and stink! Truth told time and time again—with honesty you always win!*"

After retrievin' the putty, Grandma continued, "Along the way you have lost some of our trust. Remember, when you pull Silly Putty, it breaks. Our trust in you has been broken. When that happens, it is harder and harder to gain back a person's trust."

"I want people to trust me like they trust you. I'd better get started. Can...I mean *may*...I call Momma tonight to come clean—*squeaky clean on the inside*?"

"Yes, you may. There's no time like the present!"

Grandma handed me her rotary phone and let me dial our number—94232. I told Momma to imagine me lookin' her straight in her eyes. I wanted her to see my heart. Then I told the whole truth 'n' nothin' but the truth. Momma's voice sounded pleased.

Pourin' your heart out can be so exhaustin'. I was worn out. Grandma quickly wrapped my damp hair in *Spoolies*. When she was finished, I gave her a hug and to my surprise Billy Bob, the Bed Bug, was dancin' on Grandma's toilet-papered head. I'd tell her about my new friend, but I don't think she'd believe me at this point.

"Is there something else you want to say?"

"No, not now...but do we have time for our song?"

"Always!"

Love Me, Love Me to Bed

Words and Music by
Ronda Friend

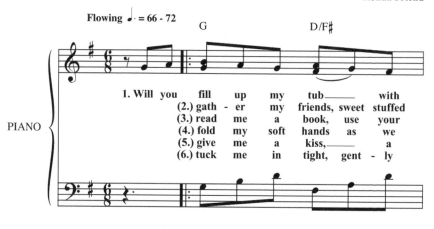

1. Will you fill up my tub_____ with
(2.) gath - er my friends, sweet stuffed
(3.) read me a book, use your
(4.) fold my soft hands as we
(5.) give me a kiss,_____ a
(6.) tuck me in tight, gent - ly

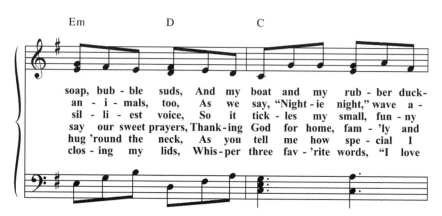

soap, bub - ble suds, And my boat and my rub - ber duck-
an - i - mals, too, As we say, "Night - ie night," wave a -
sil - li - est voice, So it tick - les my small, fun - ny
say our sweet prayers, Thank-ing God for home, fam - 'ly and
hug 'round the neck, As you tell me how spe - cial I
clos - ing my lids, Whis-per three fav - 'rite words, "I love

Prayers finished and lights out, Grandma whispered, "Ronda, you seem snug as a bug in a rug. Sleep tight! *Don't let the bed bugs bite.*"

She knows! Grandma winked, I blinked and she was gone.

Eyelids shut, I began countin' sheep – silly sheep with wool wigs on their heads. Unable to see, they'd jump over the fences, *rammin'* into each other. *Chaos and confusion ensued.* Grandma *was* right! A bunch of little lies will lead to total chaos and confusion.

Back to countin' sheep, I spotted Billy Bob, the Bed Bug, joinin' those silly sheep. He was wearin' a sheepish grin and a woolly, baaad wig!

I laughed myself to sleep.

CHAPTER 9

It's an Emergency!

Sunshine fell on Grandma's sweet halo, I mean *hat,* as she set a bouquet of pink peonies from her garden on the front seat. For the ride home, I sat in back, clutchin' onto my overnight bag. Grandma noticed I wasn't talkin' and then she asked, "Is something *bugging* you?"

Grandma knew!

"No."

Oh, no! I thought. *There I go again—another lie!*

"Are you sure nothing's *bugging* you?"

Out of the blue, Billy Bob, the Bed Bug, popped out of my bag, then looked straight at me with those buggy blue eyes! "Billy Bob, stop lookin' at me!"

He did, and then he vanished into thin air!

"Ronda, what did you say?"

"Sorry, Grandma, I was talkin' to Billy Bob."

"Oh!"

"He's really a pest—I mean, a *bug*—I mean... my conscience? I don't really know what I mean. We've just met."

"So he's your *imaginary* friend?"

75

Knowin' she might not believe me, I responded, "Yes, my *imaginary* friend who thinks I *talk* too much and *think* too little! He's tryin' to teach me things."

Lookin' in the rearview mirror, Grandma asked, "Have you learned anything from him yet?"

"Yes, to always tell the truth even if it *bugs* you to death!"

Grandma smiled. "You're home and I've an errand to run. I'll be right back!"

Diane ran outside to greet me. Distracted by a disturbance comin' from the chicken house, we both ran and took our positions. It was *hawkephant* time! Our brothers were shearin' sheep. They work together a lot, but sometimes Duane will keep *talkin' and talkin' and talkin'* 'till Ronald just can't take it any longer. This was one of those moments. The fleece was flyin' as the siblings squabbled back 'n' forth.

"Ronald, I don't know why you don't like conversations."

"A *normal* conversation is an exchange between *two* people. But a conversation with you involves one person—*you*! I can never get a word in edgewise."

"You talk just as much as I do!"

"Yeah, but when I talk, everyone *learns* something. Besides, don't you see I'm busy? Hold onto the sheep's legs. Let me focus."

"But what's wrong with talkin'?"

"Duane, you're really *getting on my nerves!*"

"Let me cut some..."

"*Cut it out!* And if you don't cut it out, *I* will!"

"But why can't I..."

"Duane, you're trying my patience! We're almost done. *Don't let her go!*"

Evidently Duane didn't hear the *"don't"* and *"did"* let go. As the shears slipped from Ronald's hand, the electric cord severed in two parts and the ends landed near the ewe's heart. The ewe cried, "Baaaa, baaa!" then whimpered.

Then there was silence.

Ronald spotted me. "Ronda, run! Daddy's in the barn!"

Legs spinnin' like never before, I hollered, "Help, Daddy! *It's an emergency! It's an emergency!*"

If anybody could help, it would be Daddy.

As Daddy and I arrived on the scene, we saw Diane tuggin' on Momma's apron, draggin' her out of the house. Puzzled, we watched three baby lambs, prancin' 'n' bleatin' nearby. Daddy calmly instructed Momma to bring some supplies. He rattled them off so quickly, all I heard was, "...water, turpentine, clean rags and a needle."

At the scene, Daddy immediately started quizzin' the boys. They quickly responded to every one of his questions. Ronald reminded Daddy that the ewe was the mother of triplets. Mystery solved. Momma and Diane arrived with the supplies as Ronald helped Daddy carefully carry the ewe to a pen in the chicken house. Momma followed.

Duane, Diane and I did the best we could to calm the triplets, knowin' all the while their momma's life was in great danger. Grandma returned as Ronald, lookin' a little down in the dumps, exited the chicken house. He gave us an update as Grandma reassured us all that with Daddy's great veterinarian skills and Momma's nursing skills, the injured ewe would be in good hands. "Remember, prayer changes things!"

We prayed and waited.

Finally, our parents came out and told us that all we could do now was to wait and pray.

The only table talk over supper was our prayers for a speedy recovery. After clearin' the dishes, Momma whispered in Daddy's ear. He instructed us that after finishin' our chores, there would be a family meeting in the girls' bedroom. We were warned *not* to go into the room until time. He concluded, "Until then, your mother and I will be caring for the ewe and her three precious lambs. Keep praying!"

What in the world was going on? Was the ewe in trouble? Were we in trouble? Did we do something wrong? None of us could figure it out.

CHAPTER 10

The Truth...and Nothing but the Truth!

The moment had arrived. We four Friends filed into my room, which had been completely rearranged. Grandma, dressed in a Sunday suit, sat behind a typewriter in front and to the left of a tall table. Momma, in her nurse's uniform, stood to the right by a chair encased in wooden slats. Instructed to take our places on the window seat, Diane, a bit bewildered, jumped in my lap.

Grandma stood and declared, "All rise—the Honorable Judge Harold Eugene Friend presiding."

We followed Ronald's lead and rose. Daddy, dressed in a black robe and an out-of-control white wig, entered the room, then sat stoically behind the tall table. Graspin' a gavel, he tapped it three times and announced, "Court is now in session. You can be seated."

Grandma whispered, "Harold, they '*may*' be seated—not '*can*' be seated!"

"Er...I stand corrected, you *may* be seated! First, the cute, I mean, the court's nurse, Jean, has an update."

"I'm happy to announce that the injured ewe is resting nicely. She is in good condition and expected to make a total recovery, due to the actions of some very brave and honest Friends. Secured in a pen next to our patient are her precious three little lambs. As of five minutes ago, all were calm, cool and collected."

"Yes, but things could change," Judge Friend interjected. "They are siblings, you know! Ha!"

Tryin' not to laugh, Momma took off her nurse's cap, turned her back to us and slipped on one of Daddy's dress shirts, jacket and tie. After placin' an old pair of Ronald's glasses on her head, she faced forward.

"She's the lawyer now," whispered Ronald.

Grandma Brombaugh stood. "By order of the Honorable Judge Harold Eugene Friend, the Friend Family has been summoned to this courtroom to hear testimony of what exactly took place to put one of *Friendly Acres's* sheep in harm's way."

"Punishment shall be decided in my chambers if for any reason a Friend tries *to pull the wool over my eyes,*" Judge Friend sternly warned. Adjustin' his wanderin' wig, he chuckled. "Besides, my wig is doing that quite well—*pulling the wool over my eyes,* that is."

Regainin' his composure, Judge Friend used two signs and a pointer to clarify his next point. "*You*—and I don't mean the *'ewe'* in question—I mean *you, you, you* and/or *you* will be punished for any *woolly baaad* lies spoken in this courtroom today!

TAP...

TAP...

TAP...

"My *saintly* court reporter will be calling you up to the stand—one by one— instructing you to lay your right hand on her Bible, the other *big book*, and you will repeat after her: 'I will tell the truth, nothing but the truth, so help me God.' Then my lovely, I mean the lawyer, will question in detail what exactly took place the afternoon of the sheep's almost fatal mishap. In closing, you will be allowed to give your testimony."

Ronald, not only the eldest but *Mr. World Bookworm Encyclopedia*, went first and answered directly every question posed to him, then added, "Father, I mean Judge Friend, I admit I get a little hot under the collar and overreact to Duane's excessive talkin' at times. I, like most Friends, love to talk too, but for the most part, it's when it's something *worthwhile* I learned from my reading."

Grandma, peckin' as fast as she could, managed to keep up with Ronald's rhetoric: "In truth, one of our dear forefathers, Thomas Jefferson, once avowed, '*Honesty is the first chapter in the book of wisdom.*' Therefore, let the records show that I believe what *honestly* happened is that Duane didn't perceive my specific instructions due, in part, to the shrill sounds of the strident shears. For instance, when I ordered, '*Don't* let go,' I believe he heard only the words *let go* and did accordingly...which reminds me of something I read in a book," Ronald rambled on.

"Son—I mean, Ronald—you need to wrap it up," Daddy interrupted. "Remember, Duane and Ronda haven't testified yet."

"So, in conclusion, I would like to thank my parents for their first aid knowledge, which, I might point out, they obtained by reading books. Let us all remember: *'If you read a lot, you know a lot!'*"

Duane, sweatin' up a storm and in the hot seat next, was under pressure. I think I saw a few hives break out on his neck—and I don't mean *bee* hives! In somewhat of a hurried fashion, he pleaded guilty to gettin' on Ronald's nerves and admitted that sometimes he talked too much. But he revealed that most of the time he was just talkin' to himself. He couldn't help it if other people just happened to be around at the time. That made the grownups chuckle!

"And, Ronald, you are correct in your observation. I didn't hear the *'don't'*, I only heard the *'do'*. I didn't mean for *any* of this to happen. I'm sorry."

I watched as my brothers embraced one another. I think I even saw a few tears—*good ones* this time. There was somethin' about watchin' my older brothers own up to their mistakes and tell everythin' without stretchin' the truth that made me proud to be their sister. I recognized then that the adult trio was attemptin' in a fun way to show how nerve-rackin' it could be if we were ever called to court to *tell the truth, nothin' but the truth, so help us, God.*

On my way to the stand, I noticed Grandma stretchin' Silly Putty. She winked as I raised my right hand and put my left hand on the Bible. My heart pounded. *"I will tell the truth, nothing but the truth, so help me, God!"*

Heart poundin', I grasped the arm of the witness chair and testified, "Your Honor, if I were the judge, I wouldn't punish anyone. If my brothers had chosen to cover things up and not get help, a very sick and injured sheep could have died. But, instead, my brothers listened to their *conscience*, told the truth and, in turn, saved a life. I'm mighty proud to be their sister. A very wise person once said, *'Lies stretch and grow then in a blink, start to spread, smell, swell and stink! Truth told time and time again—with honesty you always win!'* "

I saw Grandma's halo light up and the judge *sminked* at the lawyer. (I don't think he's allowed to do that.)

Last, but not least, Diane took the stand and before Grandma spoke a word, she mumbled, *"I woolly will twy to tell the trooth, tho help me, Gawd."*

Gigglin', Mother asked, "Diane, as a hawkephant, do you have anything to add?"

"What happened was *woolly baaaad,* but my brothers didn't do it on *porpoise*—not on *porpoise* at all. It was an accident!"

Three taps of the gavel resounded in the courtroom and Daddy proclaimed, *"Out of the mouth of babes*—this court is adjourned!"

Ronald told us to rise as the three grownups left the room. The four Friends waited patiently. *Mr. Know-It-All* informed us that they were in deliberation. Noah's definition:

---

deliberation / di-li-b -'r -sh n / noun / 2: a discussion and consideration by a number of persons of the reasons for and against a measure

---

The Four Friends stood as the trio, carryin' paper sacks, reentered the courtroom and took their places. Judge Friend asked for the verdict to be read. Grandma stood. "We, the people of the court, find the four defendants...*not guilty* of pulling the wool over their parents' eyes."

Momma asked that Ronald step forward. "Your quick, honest response saved a ewe's life," she said. "For your *perseverance* in shearing enough sheep to cover the cost of the shears, we would like to award you a small token of our appreciation."

Daddy handed him his shears, complete with a new cord. Grandma produced a pair of wool socks she had knitted. Daddy declared, "You've earned it! And for what it's worth, I do believe you have a gift for public speaking too!"

"Duane, you're next. Your father and I commend you for your display of trustworthiness. We can trust you when it comes to telling the truth. For not stretching the truth, we'd like for you to have fun stretching this!"

Momma handed him an egg carton.

"Wow, it's a whole carton of..."

"Thilly puddy," Diane guessed.

With his hand in a paper sack, Daddy laughed, "Speakin' of silly, here's a *hand* in telling the truth, the whole truth and nothing but the truth," then pulled out a cardboard replica of a hand.

Once a joker, always a joker!

Grandma motioned Duane over and presented the plastic mouse he had put in *my* overnight bag. After whisperin' secrets back and forth, Duane gave Grandma a high five with his cardboard hand.

Daddy came down from his bench as I stood anxiously at his side. "Ronda, we're proud of how you are learning the importance of *honesty*. Your mother and I appreciated the phone call last night to come clean—*squeaky clean*. The more you tell the truth, the more we can trust you to tell the truth. May you remain squeaky clean on the inside and outside," he concluded as he handed me a box of *Mr. Bubbles*.

Kissin' my cheek, Momma handed me a jar packed with Chicklets and whispered in my ear, "This is *ABC* gum—Ask *Before* Chewing."

Makin' sure no one saw, Grandma slipped a surprise in my pocket and whispered, "The mouse wasn't the only thing I saw. Don't peek until you're tucked in bed tonight, promise?"

I promised.

"My turn!" Diane shouted.

Miss Hawkephant appeared to fly into Daddy's arms while Momma spoke, "Diane, you assisted me in gathering all the supplies we needed to help doctor up that ewe. You have a heart of *compassion*. This may come in handy one day!"

Momma handed Diane her own nurse's bag complete with a play stethoscope, thermometer and candy medicine. Momma placed a tiny nurse's cap on her head as Daddy held up a special *from the bottom of my heart* note.

"We have two more surprises for each of you. Everyone close their eyes – no peeking!"

I felt somethin' placed around my neck, plus somethin' itchy on my head. Instructed to open our eyes, the Friend Family started baaaing hysterically. Everyone, including Momma and Grandma, were wearing their very own *woolly baaad* judge's wigs. And all Four Friends were wearin' homemade medals, inscribed with the words, "*Honesty is the best policy!*"

"Benjamin Franklin is noted for writing that quote," *Mr. Know-It-All* said. "In 1752, he also invented the lightning rod . . ."

"Speaking of lights," Daddy interrupted. "Lights out in five minutes. I expect each of 'ewe'— I mean, *you, you, you* and *you*—to be countin' sheep!"

Tucked in bed and tuckered out, I almost forgot my surprise. Wow, it was an exact replica of my new friend—Billy Bob. I blinked and the *real* Billy Bob, the Bed Bug, appeared.

"*That* bug *bugs* me! Where did you get that?"

"Let's just say a *little angel* gave it to me—the only one who really knows the truth about you!"

"Grandma Brombaugh *did* see me hiding in your bag. I guess she knows now that I'm just a measly, scrawny, insignificant insect—a puny, pathetic parasite."

"You are not a measly, scrawny, insignificant insect. If Grandma Brombaugh were here, she'd say, '*HOGWASH! Billy Bob the Bed Bug, you have potential!*'"

"Bug juice! I'm telling you the truth. I'm a mess except, I don't lie, you know! You really think I have potential?"

"*You can do anything you set your mind to do !*"

With Diane fast asleep, I stood and with all the gusto I could muster, I sang:

Billy Bob, the Bed Bug — my imaginary friend.

He's honest, truthful, upright –
law-abiding to the end!
Candid, frank, and decent, no bad bones
in this insect!
Just one tiny, little problem – he has no self-respect!

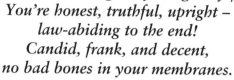

Billy Bob, the Bed Bug – my imaginary friend.
You're honest, truthful, upright –
law-abiding to the end!
Candid, frank, and decent,
no bad bones in your membranes.

Side-by-side, secret pals –
friends forever we'll remain!

I yawned and then said, "Goodnight, Billy Bob the Bed Bug. Thanks for teachin' me the importance of always tellin' the truth. We'll keep workin' on your confidence."

Billy Bob, the Bed Bug, replied, "Thanks for lifting my spirits. I feel like I could fly! Sleep tight 'n' don't let the bed bugs bite!"

I fell asleep, dreamin' that Billy Bob, the Bed Bug, dressed up as a sheep, *was* flyin'—right over fences.

Zzzzzzzzzzzzzzzzzzzzzz!

The phone rang, which woke me up. Diane and I peeked between the banisters to find Momma on the phone with Grandma. "Calm down, Mother, calm down. It's the middle of the night and Harold is on his way. I'll stay on the phone until he gets there and takes care of your *heebie-jeebies*."

Momma spotted Diane and me hoverin'. She covered the phone's mouthpiece and assured us, "Trust me, girls, everything is under control. I'm telling the truth. Grandma will be just fine. Go back to bed. I'll tell you all about it in the morning."

To find out what happens, you'll *hafta* read the next book!

Keep your eyes peeled
and look for the sunflowers!
Every full illustration in this book
has a hidden sunflower.

GRANDMA BROMBAUGH'S FAMOUS POTATO SALAD

6-7 medium potatoes   1 T salt
1 cup chopped celery   ¼ cup chopped onion
1 small jar pimentos

Peel potatoes and cut in pieces about size of a small egg.
Place potatoes in pot. Cover with cool water adding 1 T salt.
Bring to boil. After 10 minutes – or when potatoes can be easily cut with a fork (but not mushy) – drain potatoes.

DRESSING

1 cup mayonnaise — ½ cup sugar — 1 t. cider vinegar — 1 T mustard

Prepare dressing while potatoes cook. Add dressing while the potatoes are hot. Then add celery, onions and pimentos.
Mix all together and chill before serving.

Harold Eugene Friend
"Daddy off to the Toot"

Jean Vivian Friend
"Momma at the Toot"

Duane Friend
"Duane's Cuckoo Eyes"

Grandma Brombaugh
and the Boys
*"Grandma's Clean, White, Small
and Pleasant home"*

Friendly Acres
"Hauling manure - a part of farm life!"

Friend Family
"Ronda's Rockin' Horse"

Grandma's House
"Grandma's Car"

Daddy Friend
"Daddy loved to trap!"

Farmer Friend
"Reserve Champion Ewe"

Diane
"Diane and Mother Rabbit"

Friendly Acres
"Corriedale Ewe & the Triplets"

Daddy's Favorite Picture
"Grandma Friend's Favorite Picture"

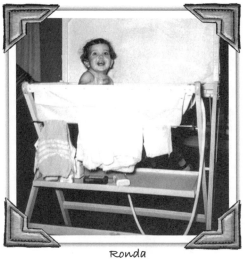

Ronda
"Squeaky Clean!"

Ronda
"Spoolies"

Diane
"Miss Hawkephant"

William Robert
"Billy Bob, the BedBug"

My Father Loves

Words and Music by
Ronda Friend

Expressively, with freedom ♩ = 100

1. Be - fore ap - pear - ing on the scene,____ he
(2.) taught me what true love is,____ he

he was wai - ting pa - tient - ly.____ Arms out-stretched, he wel-comed me with____
showed me how to live. No need for love to be re-turned, he loves

o - ver-whelm-ing pride. My help - er, con - fi - dant, pro -
lov - ing just to give. The twin - kle in his eyes, the

3rd time to Coda ⊕

liev - a - ble, my fa - ther loves. _____ My fa - ther loves, And not just for to - day, but yes - ter - day, for - ev - er I can say, my fa - ther loves. 2. He loves. A

1 | **2**

23 *Slower, freely*

thou - sand words could ne'er ex - press the love he does pos - sess. _____ And

Besides Grandma Brombaugh, What Do Other People Say About Honesty?

"No man has a good enough memory to make a successful liar." *Abe Lincoln*

"When in doubt tell the truth." *Mark Twain*

"There is no right way to do something wrong." *unknown*

"Honesty shines like the light through your eyes." *unknown*

"Peace if possible, truth at all costs." *Martin Luther King*

"A liar will not be believed, even when he speaks the truth." *Aesop*

"No legacy is so rich as honesty." *William Shakespeare*

"Honesty – the best of all the lost arts." *Mark Twain*

"Oh, what a tangled web we weave, when first we practice to deceive!" *Sir Walter Scott*

"If you tell the truth you don't have to remember anything." *Mark Twain*

"An honest answer is the sign of true friendship." *Proverb*

According to Noah . . .

Honest – free from deception, truthful, genuine, real, humble, plain, reputable, respectable, good, worthy, creditable, marked by integrity, upright, frank, sincere, innocent, simple

Honesty – implies a refusal to lie, steal or deceive in any way.

About the Author

Ronda Friend (R. Friend) is a master storyteller, musician, singer, songwriter and motivational speaker. She has captivated the hearts of hundreds of thousands of children. Administrators, teachers, parents and children describe her presentations and books as "heart-warming, energizing, hilarious, fun, sensitive, caring, entertaining and refreshing."

As author of the *Down on Friendly Acres* series, Ronda's vision is to plant seeds of a different kind – seeds of kindness, patience, laughter, perseverance and honesty into the lives of children and their families. *Woolly Baaad Lies* is the fifth book in her farm series. Her *Wild & Wacky Animal Tales* series of picture books include *P.U. You Stink!* (teamwork) and *Waddle I Do Without You!* (friendship), slated for release in 2013.

Ronda holds a B.A. degree in education with a minor in music. She has two grown children, Jeremy and Stephanie, and lives with her husband, Bill, in Franklin, Tennessee.

Check out www.RondaFriend.com for booking information.

Remember . . .
Grandma Brombaugh says,

"Lies stretch and grow then in a blink, start to spread, smell, swell and stink! Truth told time and time again—with honesty you always win!"